About the Author

ETHAN DANIEL JAMES is the creator and host of the highly popular YouTube channel THE HONEST CARPENTER. A lifelong carpenter and tradesman, he now spends much of his time writing and teaching people how to work with their hands. He lives in Greensboro, North Carolina.

Visit the author at:
www.edanieljames.com
www.youtube.com/c/thehonestcarpenter

DuNgeoNWorLd

1

DUNGEON WORLD

E. DANIEL JAMES

ONE HOT SPARK

First paperback edition 2022

Book Illustrations by Michelle Nobles

ISBN 978-1-957349-00-8 (paperback)

ISBN 978-1-957349-01-5 (ebook)

Honest Carpenter Publishing

Visit the author online!

www.edanieljames.com

For Hudson and Genevieve.
My favorite brunts.

ONE **HOT** SPARK

E. Daniel James
Illustrated by Michelle Nobles

1. The Door in the Dark

MY NAME IS Spark.

That's it. Just Spark.

My name *used* to be Thomas Redmond, and I was a totally normal 10-year-old kid. But that was before I got trapped in Dungeonworld. Now I spend my days waiting hand and foot (and *hoof*) on every goblin, ogre, and troll that comes calling!

Here's what happened…

I was hanging out with my friends, Asher and Barrett, one day after school. The final bell had just rung, and we were walking to the busses to go home.

As usual, we were talking about how awful our teacher, Mr. Henry, was.

"Whew! Mr. Henry's breath was terrible today," Asher said, scrunching his nose. "It smelled like he'd been wolfing down dead fish at lunch!"

"Yeah," Barrett added. "And his bald spot was so shiny it made my eyes hurt."

"He's got more hair growing out of his ears than his head," I said. "He looks like a goblin!"

We started laughing our guts out as we clomped down the stairs at the end of the hall. We were just about to walk outside when I noticed that a door under the stairwell was standing open.

"Hey, isn't that the door to the school basement?" I asked.

Barrett nodded.

"The janitor must have left it open."

I knew we weren't supposed to go into the basement. There was even a big sign on the door that said KEEP OUT! But I've never been too good at following rules.

I looked up and down the hallway.

"Let's sneak in!" I whispered.

"You kidding?" Asher said. "We'll get in trouble."

"No, we won't. If someone comes, we'll just hide. We can slip out when they're gone."

I could tell the guys didn't want to. But I wasn't going to let that stop me. I walked over to the door and pulled it open.

"Guess I'll see you later," I said with a wave.

It only took a second for them to come chasing after me.

"Hang on, Tom! We're not scared."

They crowded in beside me, and I pulled the door shut behind us.

"Man, it's creepy down here!" Barrett said with a shudder.

"Yeah," Asher said. "It's like a sewer."

The basement was full of pipes and old machinery. It smelled like damp and mildew. But I wasn't bothered.

"You guys are wimps," I told them. "It looks like the basement at my grandfather's house."

"Well, I wouldn't want to be in that one either," Asher grumbled.

I rolled my eyes.

Really, I got a kick out of it. I've always liked feeling braver than everyone else. A lot of kids at school called me a *daredevil* because I'm not afraid to try anything. And this basement wasn't even scary!

I was just about to say we should go when Asher pointed across the room through the darkness.

"Hey, what's that over there by the furnace?" he said.

"What?"

"That…"

I followed his finger across the room.

There, in the concrete wall, was a *second* door. It didn't look like the other doors in the school. This one was made of wood and iron, and it was studded all over with nails. A sign on the door said MORTAL PERIL.

"Mortal Peril," Asher read. "What's that mean?"

"It means danger," Barrett said. "*Extreme* danger." He scratched his head for a moment. "Who would put a door like that down here?"

"How should I know?" Asher asked, slipping behind us. "It looks all weird. Like something out of a graveyard."

Even I had to admit the door did look a little weird. There were scratches in the wood, sort of like claw marks.

"I think we should just go to the bus lot," Asher said.

"I agree," Barrett added.

But I was too curious to walk away now.

I moved a little closer to inspect the door. I wondered if Mr. Renfrow, the janitor, even knew about it. Surely, he would have mentioned it to the principal by now. They would have bricked it over or something.

I got the feeling the door was trouble. But I'd never been able to walk away from a mystery, and this was a mystery of the highest order.

"Let's open it," I said.

"What!" Asher said. "Are you crazy?"

"Yeah, it says 'mortal peril,' Thomas. That can't be a good sign."

I brushed off their worries.

"Come on. It can't be *that* bad. We're in school, for crying out loud!"

"Yeah, but I don't think that door is part of the school," Barrett said.

"Then what's it doing here?"

"Making me uncomfortable," he groaned.

I stood there, trying to decide if I should open the door or not.

You already opened one forbidden door, I thought. *A second one can't hurt, right?*

I made up my mind.

"You guys better stand back," I said.

Barrett and Asher went scrambling away as I grabbed the black iron handle and pulled. The door was heavy as could be—I had to pull with all my strength. I ground my teeth and grunted.

KRRRACK!

A seal of dirt broke, and the door swung open in my hand. A gust of cold, stinking air came whooshing out.

"Ugh, it smells awful in there!" I said, waving a hand in front of my face.

Barrett peeked over my shoulder.

"What's inside?" he asked timidly.

I gazed into the dark.

I couldn't see a thing. Just blackness.

I shook my head.

"I think it's empty," I said.

"Let's get out of here then!" Asher said.

"Yeah, Thomas," Barrett said. "Let's scram. This place is giving me the creeps!"

I couldn't leave just yet, though. I was too curious.

"I'm going to look just a little closer," I said.

I inched towards the door as a wisp of smoke crept out along the floor. I thought I could see something in there now—a shape moving around in the dark.

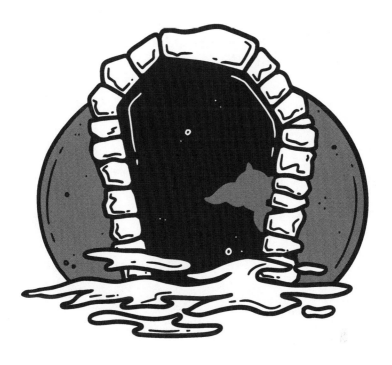

I glanced back over my shoulder.

"I think there's someone in here," I hissed.

It turned out those would be the last words I'd speak in the human world.

A skinny, warty green arm shot out from the shadowy doorway and grabbed the front of my shirt. It snatched me clean off my feet and dragged me headlong into the darkness.

The last thing I heard was the sound of Asher and Barrett screaming their heads off. Then, the heavy door slammed shut behind me...

2. Mortal Peril

I T WAS PITCH black around me. I tried to pry apart the bony knuckles gripping my shirt, but they were too strong.

A rattling, nasty voice spoke.

"Okay, let's have a look at you then…"

Torches flared to life. Suddenly, I was staring up into the ugliest face I'd ever seen.

Yellow eyes gazed down at me over a long, skinny nose. Huge, pointy ears stuck out of a green, lumpy head. Glistening red teeth hung through cracked lips.

"W-what are y-you?" I asked.

"What's it look like?" the creature said. "I'm a goblin, ain't I? Not too smart, this one…"

I couldn't believe it. I'd just accused Mr. Henry of looking like a goblin, and here I was staring at a real, living goblin! I would have taken Mr. Henry's face over this one any day of the week.

"Let go of me!" I shouted.

I fought and kicked and punched to break free, but the bony hands wouldn't let go. The goblin just laughed a stinking breath straight into my face.

"We've got a live one here, Judge!" he cackled.

Across the room, an old, wheezy voice spoke.

"They all come through that way. Hot and bothered. No sense, humans."

I looked over into the shadows. A stumpy old goblin was standing there with a scroll in his hands. He had huge ears like batwings. His eyebrows were so bushy he couldn't even see out from under them.

We were in a stuffy little room. The walls and floor were made of hard, gray stone. It stank like rotted vegetables in here.

"Where am I?" I asked.

"Where do you think?" the skinny goblin spat. "You're in Mortal Peril. Didn't you read the sign over the door?"

"Yeah, but...what's Mortal Peril?"

"It's the waiting room to Dungeonworld.

Where you'll be soon enough if you quit bothering us with silly questions!"

Dungeonworld? Waiting room?!

I didn't like the sound of any of this...

"I'd rather just go back through the door," I said anxiously.

"Oh yeah? What door?"

"That one..." I said, pointing behind me.

But when I looked back over my shoulder, I got a nasty shock. The door was gone! There was just a cold, stone wall where it had been. The goblin let out another cackling laugh.

"Too late for that now! Nobody leaves Mortal Peril once they enter."

"But...I didn't know what I was getting into!"

"Then you shouldn't have opened the door, should you?"

He had me there. I cursed myself for being too curious. I shouldn't have tried to look so brave and tough back there in the basement. Typical Thomas Redmond!

"Let's get on with this, shall we?" the old goblin said.

He opened the big, dusty scroll, then took out a pen that looked like it was made of bone. He cleared his throat loudly.

"How tall is the boy?" he asked.

The skinny goblin poked me.

"How tall is you?"

"Uhh…four feet, five inches."

"Feet and inchworms? Quite talking nonsense! Tell me in *lashers*."

"I-I don't know what lashers are."

He sighed like I was a numbskull.

"Find out myself then," he said.

He reached into his leather shirt and pulled out a piece of rope with knots in it. He held the rope up next to me and squinted at it, counting under his breath.

"I'd call it…seven lashers and sixteen licks."

The old goblin— the Judge—made a note with his bone pen.

"And what color is his hair?"

"Mud-colored, I'd say."

"And his ears? Are they large or small?"

"Puny, mate. Just puny."

The Judge shook his head and mumbled.

"No good, no good…"

The skinny goblin plucked and poked and pulled at me with his green fingers for a few minutes. The Judge tisked and sighed like I was a big disappointment.

"What's with all the questions?" I asked.

"We're trying to figure out what work you're cut out for in Dungeonworld," the skinny goblin said.

"*Work?* I don't want to work."

"Well, that's too bad! Work is all humans is good for. Now stand still, and let us finish."

"He's too small for a soldier," the Judge said, scratching his big ear. "Too testy for a cook. Too simple for a banker…"

The skinny goblin picked something from his teeth and flicked it away.

"What do you reckon we should do with him?"

"Just send him

down to Thoracks, I suppose," the Judge said. "Let him sort it out."

"Up you get then!"

The skinny goblin yanked me to my feet and started shoving me across the room.

"Where are you sending me?" I asked.

"You heard the Judge! We're sending you down to see Thoracks. And don't give him any grief, or he'll smush you flatter than bug jelly."

I swallowed a big lump in my throat. *Why did you open that door?* I thought.

The skinny goblin pushed me over to the far wall where the torches were mounted. In the flickering yellow light, I saw that there were a bunch of holes in the stone floor. They were labeled with red letters, like mail slots: THE MINES, THE ROOKERY, THE KITCHENS…

He shoved me clear down to the end. We stopped at a hole labeled ANYBODY'S GUESS.

"Say hi to old Thoracks for me," the skinny goblin said, breathing onions into my face. "And if he decides to eat you, tell him to save me some tasty parts!"

Then he picked me right up like a sack and hung my feet over the hole.

"Wait, no!" I shouted.

But he dropped me without another word. All I could do was scream as I plunged down through the darkness...

3. Thoracks

"**A**AAGH!"

My voice echoed all around me. I was on some sort of stone slide, whizzing downward at a hundred miles per hour. I twisted this way and that, bouncing between rocky walls.

It felt like I was falling for minutes. Just when I thought it would never end, a light appeared below me. I shot out of a hole like a bullet.

WHUMP!

"Ooof!"

I socked down into a deep, raspy pile of hay. For a moment, I was completely buried. Then a big hand reached in and yanked me out by the collar and set me on my feet.

"Sorry about that…the chute is a bit rough."

I gawked at the huge figure standing above me. He was dark blue and bulging with muscles. He had massive hooves for feet and big horns on his forehead. His face looked like a cross between a dog and a bull.

"Are you... *Thoracks?*" I asked.

"In the flesh! Welcome to my office."

He waved his big paw around a well-lit room. It was nicer in here than Mortal Peril. There was a big stone desk, draperies on the wall, and rugs on the floor. A fire crackled in a hearth in the corner.

"Care for some tea?" he asked, turning around to show a bull's tail poking from his pants.

"Uhh, no thanks," I said. "You're not going to eat me, are you?"

"*Me?* Of course not! Who told you that?"

"The goblin who threw me down the hole."

"Runce?" Thoracks let out a deep, rumbling laugh. "He's just getting your goat. I haven't eaten anyone in ages! I just help new folks find jobs nowadays."

He waved me to a big iron chair. I calmed down a little as I took my seat. But I was still amazed by Thoracks.

"What are you exactly?" I asked, looking him up and down as he sat behind his desk.

"I'm an ogre," he said proudly. "One of many ogres down here in Dungeonworld."

"And...what is Dungeonworld?"

"Why, it's where we live, of course! And now, it's where you live too."

Panic started to swell up in me again.

"But I don't *want* to live in Dungeonworld."

"How do you know? You haven't even seen the place yet!"

"I don't care," I said. "I'd rather just go home."

Thoracks raised an eyebrow at me.

"You sure about that? I mean, you opened to door to Mortal Peril. Surely, you must have wanted *something* more than home."

He did have a point. I could have just walked away back there in the basement, but I didn't. At the time, it had seemed like an adventure. I guess it still sort of did...in a terrifying way.

Thoracks put his fingertips together and spun lightly in his chair.

"Just wait till you see the sights," he said. "Endless chambers of stone! Bottomless pits! Ghouls, goblins, and ghosts of all descriptions!"

"Sounds…interesting," I said.

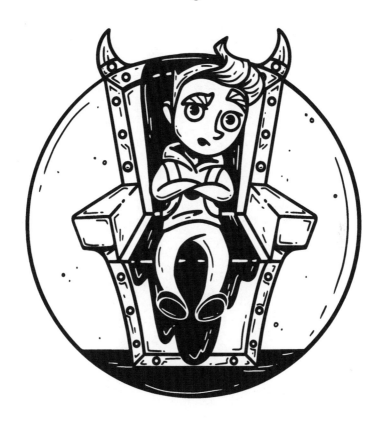

"Doesn't it?" He swiveled back around and leaned his elbows on the desk. "First thing's first, though. We've got to give you a name. Can't have you walking around like a Jack Nobody."

"I already have a name, though," I piped up. "It's Thom—"

"Ack! Don't say it," Thoracks pleaded, cringing. "I've got a full stomach, don't I? Nothing nastier than human names."

I scoffed.

"Says the guy with a dog's butt for a face…"

I regretted the words as soon as they came out. *Why can't you keep your big mouth shut, Thomas?*

I thought for sure Thoracks was going to gore me. But a little smile actually spread across lips, and he laughed another rumbling laugh.

"I like you," he said. "You've got a little *fire* in your belly. You're gonna fit right in down here."

Two thin jets of smoke slipped out of his nose as he looked me up and down. Then a light flashed in his eyes, and he snapped his fingers loudly.

"That's it! I've got it the perfect name for you."

"Really? What is it?"

"Spark!" he said.

"Spark?"

"Spark…"

I ran it through my head a few times. *Spark.*

I had to admit, I didn't hate it.
In fact, I thought it suited all my best qualities.
Thoracks must have thought so, too, because he hopped out of his seat and walked a lap around his desk. The ideas seemed to be flowing.

"And I reckon I know just the place for a young man of your talents," he said. "I'm sending you to work with the smithies!"

"The *who?*"

"The blacksmiths. The forgers of metal and steel. It's the hottest, most back-breaking work in all of Dungeonworld!"

He said this like it was some sort of good thing. I tried to argue. I *hated* hard work. But before I could get a word out, he pulled a rope hanging in the corner. A bell chimed some-where, and a steel gate opened in the wall.

Noise spilled in from a hallway outside. The grossest creature I'd seen yet came limping through the door. He was gray and pale and rotting all over. His skin was hanging off him in tatters.

"You *raaang*, sir?"

"Spark, this is Fetrol, my top ghoul," Thoracks said. "Fetrol, this is Spark. He's starting work with the smithies tomorrow. Take him down to the Pit and get him set up with lodgings."

FETROL

"Right away, sir," Fetrol said.

The ghoul slouched quickly across the room, bringing a stink of rotten shoes and spoiled fruit with him. He took me by the wrist with a soft, stringy hand.

"This way, young man," he said, yanking me to my feet.

"I'll be keeping an eye on you, Spark," Thoracks called after us. "Mind your manners here in Dungeonworld. And don't cause any trouble, or you'll be back here answering to me!"

Fetrol was dragging me out of the door. I had no choice but to go with him.

It looked like I was about to see Dungeonworld at last. Like it or not.

4. Stroll With a Ghoul

WE WALKED OUT of Thorack's office into a long stone hallway. Right off the bat, I was almost stomped to death by what looked like a passing tree trunk.

"Easy, there!" Fetrol said, yanking me out of the way just in time.

I gazed up to see a giant brown shape go scraping its head along the stone ceiling. The ground shook with every step of its meaty feet. It looked back at me with yellow eyes and a big, rocky jaw.

"**Watch it, brunt,**" it said with a voice as deep as a canyon.

I had to blink and shake my head.

"Was that a..."

"Troll," Fetrol said, watching it go. "Best to avoid them. They're rather mean and not terribly bright."

"What did it call me, though?"

"A *brunt*," Fetrol said. "A human servant in Dungeonworld."

"You mean—there are more humans like me?"

"Of course! We've got all types down here, don't we? Come along now!"

I wanted to ask when I could meet some more humans, but Fetrol was dragging me by the hand again. Soon we were limping through so many hallways and chambers that I couldn't keep my head from whipping around.

Look at this place! I thought.

I had seen castles and dungeons in movies before. But you could take the hundred biggest and best, and they couldn't touch Dungeonworld.

It was like an underground city made of stone and metal! Everywhere you looked, there were massive rooms with vaulted arches and ceilings. Fountains and rivers carried sloshing water by our feet. Torches and fire pits blew flames and swirling ash into the air.

Ogres and goblins and trolls were moving in every direction. Some wore squeaking leather clothes. Others wore clanking metal armor. They were all talking, laughing, and snorting at each other.

"Biswold, bring the ringbolts I ordered, you awful blinker…"

"Bats and rats! Get 'em while they're hot and fresh…"

"All ghoul miners, report to the lift number two-thousand-fourteen…"

Fetrol dragged me right through it all with hardly a glance back. He was fast for a dead guy! I worried one of his fingers might pop off, he was pulling me so hard.

"How big is Dungeonworld?" I shouted to him.

"Endless, young man. Just endless."

"Then…where are we going?"

"Didn't you hear Thoracks? To the Pit! It's just ahead now, keep up…"

He led us to a giant gate, and we crammed into a long, low passage with a pack of goblins.

It was a real stampede in here. Their shrieky voices echoed off the low ceiling, and it smelled like onions and soot and sweat. They hissed in my ears, poked me with their dagger-like fingernails.

I thought I'd be squeezed to death! But, finally, the crowd thinned out, and we popped through a gate on the far side. Suddenly, we were in a space so big I almost got dizzy.

"Welcome to the Pit!" Fetrol said with a wave of his jiggling arm. "Home sweet home."

It looked like we were standing in the center of a steep, gigantic stadium. Staircases and ramps and ladders rose upward and upward to a hundred different levels.

Thousands of torches and candles burned up there. Flags and ragged banners hung over doorways. Bats and ravens whipped and zipped through all the open space.

"I hope you've got strong legs," Fetrol said. "*Up we go…*"

He led me to a nearby staircase, and we started climbing our way upward, slowly winding around the big courtyard at the center.

I gawked at every room we passed. Some were as big as gymnasiums. Others were just little hutches the size of hotdog stands carved out of the rocky wall.

When we'd done a full circle around the courtyard and climbed too many levels to count, Fetrol finally stopped.

"Ahh, here we are...I knew we'd find an empty nest somewhere."

We were standing in front of the tiniest little room yet. It was just a notch in the wall with a musty curtain hanging in front. Fetrol yanked the curtain back to reveal a cramped bed with a little stone shelf above it.

"I'm supposed to live *here*?" I asked.

"Yep! Ain't it something?"

He spun around and looked out over the sprawling courtyard below us.

"What a view," he exclaimed. "The Pit's never looked so glorious!"

I could have thought of a lot of words for the view from my new doorstep, but *glorious* wasn't one of them. *Strange* might have described it better.

My head was reeling with questions. I struggled to pull my thoughts together.

"Fetrol…is this really it?" I asked. "I'm just stuck in Dungeonworld *forever*?"

"Oh no, of course not!" Fetrol said. "Human servants are allowed to leave eventually."

"Well, how long is 'eventually?'"

"However long it takes for you to do your fair share of work…or perish in a terrible accident. Whichever comes first."

My heart sank. I wondered what he meant by "fair share." But before I could ask, Fetrol reached into his torn shirt and drew out a small hourglass on a rope.

"Oh dear, time is flying," he said. "I really must be getting on."

"But…what about me?"

"Just relax! Enjoy yourself! Work doesn't start till morning. A young man's got to have some fun in his free time."

Fun? *In this place?* I was surrounded by deadly ogres and goblins. Who could think of fun right now? Fetrol wasn't sticking around to explain, though. He began slouching off with a creaking of bones and muscles.

"Best of luck at the smithy tomorrow, Spark... *Ta ta!*"

Like that, I was alone in Dungeonworld.

5. The Shakylegs

I DIDN'T KNOW WHAT to do with myself, so I turned around and flopped down on my sad, lumpy bed.

"Ouch!"

Something hard poked me in the back.

I reached under myself and searched through the covers. I pulled out a skinny, yellow bone. It looked like part of a leg. Property of the last guy to sleep in this bunk.

"Good grief," I muttered. "Somebody will

probably be pulling *my* bones out of this bed one day."

I sighed and tossed the bone onto my stony porch, where it rattled and clanked. I lay there with my arms over my face for a while, moping.

Some daredevil you are, Thomas Redmond, I thought. *A real tough guy!*

But something funny occurred to me…

My name wasn't Thomas Redmond anymore.

It was *Spark.*

Thomas Redmond might have been scared of this place. But Spark didn't necessarily have to be. Maybe Spark *belonged* in Dungeonworld.

I rolled over and hung my legs out of the bunk. I looked at all the flickering lights out there in the Pit. Fetrol was right, it did look sort of pretty in a way. Maybe it was all just a matter of how you looked at things.

How often do you get to visit a place like Dungeonworld? I thought. *Are you just going to lay around complaining? Or are you going to get out there and explore!*

I suddenly felt a new burst of energy.

I sprang up out of my bed and set out walking with a little pep in my step.

"And if you get into any trouble, just do what the locals do," I told myself. "Act like you own the place!"

I walked up the winding pathway until I came to a raucous tavern. I stopped just outside the place and stood looking in. Smoke and fumes were pouring out of the dim chamber, along with loud, howling voices.

A sign over the door said *THE SHAKYLEGS.*

Seems like a pretty fun place, I thought.

The problem was, two huge trolls were standing on either side of the doorway with their arms crossed. I tried to walk in between them, but the troll on the right stopped me with a finger like a battering ram.

"Oi! What do you think you're doin'? No brunts allowed inside!"

Now, Thomas Redmond probably would have gone running straight back to the hutch in a moment like this. But Spark played it cool.

"I'm not a brunt," I said like I was offended. "I'm a king!"

"Oh yeah? Of what?"

I thought for a second.

"Grimvale Elementary," I said. That was my old school.

The troll sneered.

"Ain't never heard o' the place!"

"I'm not surprised. It's totally boring," I said.

Then I made my eyes real big and pointed up like I was terrified. "Woah! You've got a huge *brain-for* on your head!"

"**Blimey! What's a brain for?**" he said, grabbing his bald dome. He turned to his partner. "**Hey mate, what's a brain for?!**"

"**Search me. Hunker down, and I'll have a look…**"

They started searching for the invisible brain-for. I took the opportunity to slip between them. No problems.

I walked straight into a packed tavern. Ogres and goblins were strewn across every booth, bench, and barstool. They were banging wooden mugs on tables, slinging darts through the smoky gloom. A two-headed dog chewed an ox bone in the corner.

"Wow!" I said. "This place is great!"

I was looking for a quiet corner to hide out in when a sharp whistle cut through the noise.

"Hey! You're a little short to be in here, aren't you?"

I looked to my left to find an ogre cleaning glasses behind a granite bar. This ogre wasn't nearly as ugly as the other ones, though. In fact, this ogre was sort of...*pretty.*

A lady ogre, I thought.

She had blonde hair and big red lips, and she was eyeing me with a funny grin. I struggled to think up some excuse for how I'd gotten in, but she just laughed.

"Don't sweat it, kid. Come belly up to the bar!"

I walked over, climbed onto an empty barstool, and hung my elbows over the high counter. She set the glass aside.

"What's your name then?" she asked.

"Spark."

"Pleased to meet you, Sparky. I'm Caledonia. What can I get for you?"

"Uhh…what do you have?" I asked.

"Let's see," she said, searching around the bar. "Pickled onion…fried bat wings… fricasseed rat tail…tender pig's ear…moldy mushrooms…"

My nose scrunched up. None of that sounded like anything I wanted to eat. But I was starving, so I said, "Pickled onion, I guess."

Caledonia fished a few slimy, purple onions out of a big jar and handed them to me on a pointed stick. I took a bite of one. It actually wasn't that bad, as long as I held my breath.

"New to the neighborhood?" she asked.

I swallowed a mouthful of onion.

"Yeah. It's my first day."

"Takes some getting used to," she said. "Where you working?"

"With the blacksmiths."

"Gor! That's a plum of a job!" Caledonia said. "How'd you get that one?"

"Some ogre named Thoracks gave it to me."

Caledonia nodded wisely.

"Good bloke, Thoracks. Just don't go making him mad, though. He's got a temper like a ninety-pound cannon. Want to try some bat wing?"

"Sure!"

Caledonia ended up serving me everything on the menu. I crunched my way through helpings of rat tail and barbecue frog legs. The whole time, trolls arm-wrestled at the long wooden tables, and goblins played *dart dodgers* against the back wall.

Time must've flown right by. Before I knew it, Caledonia was ringing a big bell over the bar.

"Closing time, you thundering lumps! Come pay your bills, or I'll break your thumbs!"

There was a big rush to the bar as goblins and ogres started tossing copper and gold coins onto the countertop.

I panicked.

"Caledonia," I said nervously. "I don't have any money. I haven't worked yet!"

She waved me off with a carefree hand.

"It's on me, Sparky," she said. "Come back and see me again sometime. We'll settle up."

"Wow!" I said. "Thanks!"

I hopped off my barstool and managed to slip out without getting stepped on.

With a full belly, I felt like a whole new kid. I strolled back to my hutch, feeling sleepy and content.

Maybe Dungeonworld isn't so bad after all, I thought.

I curled up on my lumpy bed, yanked the curtain shut, and was out like a light.

6. Late For Work

MUST HAVE SLEPT like a rock. The next thing I knew, someone was poking me and shouting, "*Wake up!*"

"Leave me alone, Mom," I grumbled. "I don't want to go to school today..."

"I don't want to go to school today, either," the voice said. "And quit calling me *Mom!*"

I opened my eyes to see a human boy standing above my bed. His face was smudged with dirt, and his orange hair was sticking out in every direction like he'd been electrocuted. I sat up and swung my legs out of the bed.

"Are you a brunt?" I asked.

"What do I look like? A troll?"

No, I thought. *You just look crazy.*

"What's your name?" I said.

"It's Fits."

I made a face.

"Why do they call you—"

His head whipped back suddenly. He tried to throw an arm across his mouth, but it was too late.

"ACHOOO! ACHOOO! ACHOOO! "

"Oh," I said, wiping sneeze matter out of my eye. "Nevermind."

"Sorry....it's da mold...it gibs me allergies."

He rubbed his red nose and sniffled until he could talk normally again.

"You have to get up," he demanded. "You're late for work at the smithy! They sent me down here just to get you."

Shoot! I'd forgotten all about work. The last

thing I wanted to do right now was to go sweat it out at a blacksmith's forge.

"Do I have to go?" I asked.

Fits nodded gravely.

"If you don't show up," he said. "You might as well chuck yourself off this ledge."

I looked at the steep drop-off beyond my doorstep. I scratched my chin for a moment.

"I'm thinking…" I said.

"Just get up!"

He grabbed me by the front of my shirt. Next thing I knew, this perfect stranger was dragging me down the stone walkway towards the Pit courtyard far below.

It looked like I finally had to go to work.

"Hurry!" Fits said, zipping between lumbering gray bodies on the ramps. "We have to get there quick, or Redbone will kill us!"

"Who's Redbone?" I panted, ducking under a troll's elbow.

"He's the head blacksmith. He takes his job way too seriously. He'll pinch you with hot tongs if you make him mad."

Great! Another angry monster to deal with, I thought.

But I'd decided the night before I wasn't

going to worry too much in Dungeonworld. I'd just have to handle this Redbone when he showed up.

I was more curious about this Fits kid. He was about my age, but he looked like he'd been down here for a while. I figured I could pick his brain a little.

"How long you been in Dungeonworld?" I asked him.

"Oh, I don't know…about an eon."

"How long's an eon?"

"Somewhere between a year and a century."

I pulled my collar with a finger.

"Geez. They've sure got a funny way of keeping time down here, don't they?"

"You've got no idea! There are twenty-seven different weekdays in Dungeonworld. I still don't know them all yet. But it doesn't really matter anyway, because you can't tell one day from another. No sunlight…"

"Yeah, I noticed," I said, looking at the torches flickering in the gloomy dark. "Have you met other brunts like us?"

"Oh, sure. We're all over the place. You just have to keep your eyes peeled. And don't get squished!"

He yanked my arm just as a hay cart pushed by a fat goblin came barreling up the pathway. A cloud of hayseed wafted out as it passed us. Fits had a fit.

"ACHOOO! ACHOOO! ACHOOO!"

I'd managed to avoid getting sprayed this time. I waited for him to get his bearings, then we set out again.

"Must be tough having allergies like that," I said.

"Id was worse in da real world," Fits said, rubbing his nose. "Up there, I was allergic to *grass*."

"Well, I guess there's a bright side to everything, huh?"

"Yeah, even in a place with no sun! Come on, we're almost there."

7. The Blacksmith's Shop

WE CROWDED BACK through the Pit gate, and Fits took me down a series of winding side tunnels. Eventually, we came to a wide iron bridge over a thrashing, raging river. Fits pointed to a glowing chamber on the other side.

"That's the smithy," he said.

I looked over to see big, sweaty bodies moving beyond the doors and windows of the blacksmith's shop. The smell of burning coal drifted over to us. I could already hear the clash of ringing metal.

CLING! CLONG! BLANG!

A loud, scary voice rose above it all.

"Strunk, if you move my anvil again, you'll be wearing it for a hat!"

"That's Redbone," Fits said anxiously. "Brace yourself. He's about to let you have it."

"Should have brought my earplugs," I said under my breath.

We went jogging across the bridge. For a moment, the cool river air wafted up from below. Then, we were in the blacksmith's shop, and there was nothing *cool* about it.

I'd never been in such a hot place before! Fires roared on every side. Hot, stinky ogres clopped across the stone floor on hooves with metal shoes. There was so much sharp, gleaming metal standing around, you could slice and dice a fish just by tossing it through the air!

"Fits! What took you so bleedin' long?" the angry voice shouted. "Yer the slowest brunt in Dungeonworld!"

The shortest ogre I'd yet seen came stomping over to us. He was only half the size of Thoracks, but he seemed ten times as mean. His skin was as red as a pepper, and he was smudged all over with soot. He had a grizzly black beard on his bullish face and a big, gold ring through his nose.

REDBONE

"Sorry, sir!" Fits said. "The Pit was crowded…"

Redbone clomped over and stuck his snout in my face.

"You the one been holding up my workday?"

"I guess so."

"I guess so, *SIR!*" he barked. "What's your name then?"

I cleared my throat.

"Spark...sir."

"Well, *Spark,* we only got two rules around here. Don't be late, and don't make me mad. You ain't worked for me ten seconds, and you've already broke both of them! What do you have to say for yourself?"

I'd say Thoracks set me up with the wrong job, I thought. But I had a feeling Redbone would toss me in the river if I said it out loud. So, I just turned my eyes down to my feet.

"Sorry, sir. Won't happen again."

"Dang right it won't! Now, you brunts get to work feeding the fires. And don't give me no more trouble, or I'll use you for coals!"

"Yes, sir," we both said.

He turned away, his hooves clanking on the stone floor. Fits let out a deep breath.

"Welcome to the smithy," he said. "Come on, I'll show you how everything works."

Fits led me through the shop.

It was so cluttered I had to belly dance just to avoid everything. There were racks of new axes, hammers, swords, maces, and knives along the walls. Blacksmithing tools hung from beams and posts everywhere. Scrap metal lay in big, twisted piles.

We stopped at an enormous wooden water

tank. This thing was the size of a swimming pool, and it had a big spigot at the bottom.

"This is the cistern," Fits said, thumping the wooden wall. "It refills the cooling troughs when the water gets turned to steam. Watch…"

An ogre blacksmith came clomping over with a red-hot iron in his tongs. He swung it down into one of the stone water troughs, which erupted with a hiss.

KSSSSHHHH!

A cloud rose around him. He carried the cool iron away. Fits turned the spigot to let more water into the trough. Then, he turned it off again.

"Let's head back to the forge," he said. "That's where the real work gets done…"

He led me to a big, black object at the back of the shop. It looked like an oven you could cook a whole cow in! The thing gave off so much heat I started sweating on the spot.

Ogres were turning metal pokers on a bed of white-hot coals in the forge. When the pokers were glowing red, the ogres swung them onto anvils and pounded them into shapes with heavy hammers.

Cling! Clong! Blang!

"The forge fire has to stay hot enough to make the metal glow!" Fits shouted over the noise. "That's where we come in."

He led me around to the far side of the forge. There was an enormous pile of coal back here and another pile of ash. A big tool that looked like an accordion was poking into a hole at the bottom of the forge.

"What is that thing?" I asked.

"It's a bellows," Fits said. "It blows air into the fire when you pump it. The fire gets crazy hot that way. Watch…"

He grabbed the bellows' top handle with both hands. Clenching his jaw, he pulled down hard. The bellows wheezed out a stream of air.

WHOOSH!

The coals blazed into white flames. A gust of heat washed over my face.

"See how it works?" Fits said, dusting his hands off.

"I think so…"

"Good. Your job today is to work the bellows. I'm going to shovel in fresh coal and scoop out ash. But we have to work fast to keep it hot, so no slacking off! Ready?"

"Not really…"

"*Too bad.* Let's get to work!"

8. Feeding the Forge

I COULD TELL FITS had spent a lot of time working in the smithy. He slung fresh loads of coal into the forge lickety-split and carefully scooped out the hot cinders and ash with a flick of the shovel.

I, on the other hand, was struggling from the start…

The billow pump was as stiff as a diving board! I had to use all my weight just to pull the handle down, and it sprang back up so fast it nearly socked me in the jaw every time. My shoulders ached after just a few minutes.

Fits watched me with an impatient look.

"Pump harder!" he said. "You're letting the fire cool down."

"I'm pulling as hard as I can," I grunted.

He wasn't the only irritated one. The ogre blacksmiths on the other side were scowling at me through the forge window. Their pokers weren't glowing as brightly.

"Throw yer back into it, you measly brunt! The fire's a-dwindlin'…"

Come do it yourself then, you overgrown warthog! I thought.

I gripped the handle and started pumping the billows as hard as I could. Slowly, the fire started to glow again…

I was sweating buckets after ten minutes. My shoulders were screaming in agony, and I could already feel blisters forming on my hands. I was so dizzy I was starting to lose focus.

There's no way I'll be able to keep this up all day, I thought. *I'll die pulling this handle down! There has to be a better way…*

Out of desperation, I stopped pumping for a moment and just stepped back.

"What are you doing, Spark?!" Fits said.

"Hang on a second," I told him.

I inspected the billows with an inventor's eye. The pump was held in place by a big iron bracket that looked sturdy enough for me to stand on. It gave me an idea.

Putting my foot on the bracket, I climbed

onto the billows and balanced on the paddle-shaped handle like it was a big skateboard.

Summoning all my energy, I jumped up and drove the paddle down with my feet...

WHOOOOSH!

The biggest gust of air yet came out. The fire in the forge flared to life, white and blazing.

"Woah!" I shouted as the handle sprang back up and almost bucked me off.

Fits had stopped working for a moment to watch me. His eyes suddenly got big.

"Do it again!" he said.

I jumped again. Twice.

WHOOOOSH! WHOOOOSH!

The fire blazed even brighter. The heat from the forge licked my face.

"That's the stuff, you wee blinker!" an ogre yelled.

Fits quickly got back to work, slinging shovel loads of coal. I kept right on pumping with my feet.

It felt like I was on a surfboard in a big, rough ocean. Every time I drove the billows down, it bucked me right back up again.

This is great! I thought. *I could do this all day!*

Now the tables were turned. Fits was running back and forth between the forge, the ash pile, and the coal pile as fast as he could. His shovelhead was flying, and his cheeks were puffed out with effort.

"Slow down a little!" he said, gasping. "I can't scoop the ash fast enough!"

"I can't pump any slower this way," I told him. "I have to keep a rhythm. Just go faster!"

Fits put his head down and shoveled like a mad man. But he couldn't keep up.

The fire was blazing by this point. Ash was piling up, and cinders were starting to float around. I jumped a little too hard on the paddle once, and the billows sent an enormous gust into the fire.

WHOOOOOOOSH!

A cloud of loose ash blew out the far side of the forge. Sparks danced and swirled in the air. I watched as one big, fat spark did a spiral and landed right on the neck of an ogre pounding his metal at the anvil.

"YEEOW!"

The ogre leaped into the air, swatting at the back of his neck. When the cinder was out, he spun around with a murderous look.

"Oi!" he said to another ogre walking by. "Watch where yer stickin' yer hot poker!"

"Mind who yer barkin' at!" the ogre replied. "I ain't did nothin' wrong."

"Sneaking liar! Let's see how you like it…"

He jabbed the innocent ogre with his red-hot iron. The victim howled, then jabbed back with his own iron. Soon, it was an all-out fight! The two of them were swinging pokers and slamming into things and calling each other awful names.

"Yer a twin-handled bindlesnipe!"

"Ay? Well, yer a half-cracked goblin's helmet!"

A big troll carrying scrap metal nearby came thundering over to break it up.

"You two knock it off, or I'll gobsmack the both of ya!"

I narrowed my eyes at him. I hadn't been in Dungeonworld long, but I already didn't like trolls. They just seemed like bullies. I grinned as I gave the handle another hard pump with my feet.

WHOOOOSH!

A big puff of sparks blew straight up into his craggy face.

"**Blimey!**" the troll shouted.

He covered his eyes and went stumbling backward. I almost burst out laughing. But then his heel caught an anvil, and he came down with a thump...

Right into the ash heap!

Suddenly, everything wasn't quite so funny anymore.

9. The Fire and the Flood

POOOOF!

ASH EXPLODED into the air. It filled the blacksmith's shop like a cloud and blotted out the torches.

Poor Fits was standing right there when the troll dusted the place. He spun around and covered his mouth, but his face started twitching and twisting.

"You alright?" I asked him.

"My all...my aller..."

His head flew back, and he launched into his worst sneezing fit yet.

"ACHOOO! ACHOOO! ACHOOO!"

Soon, everyone else was coughing and shouting in confusion. Redbone came storming over, his hooves shooting sparks on the stones.

"What's goin' on over here? Knock it off, you daft blinkers! Get that troll up...clean this mess." He turned and saw me and Fits through the forge. "And you two...*keep working!*"

Fits' eyes bulged. He swallowed his sneezes and tried to get back to work. But his eyes were too watery to see through. I watched helplessly as he scooped out a load of hot ash and cinders—and tossed it straight onto the coal pile!

"Hey!" I shouted. "Watch what you're doing."

It was too late, though. The fresh coal started to smoke. Then a little blue flame crept over the pile. It quickly turned into a bright yellow flame.

Right before my eyes, the whole mountain of coal started burning!

Fits was trying to toss another shovel load on when I jumped down from the billows and grabbed him.

"Stop," I shouted. "It's on fire!"

"Fire?" he said. "Where?"

"Right in front of you, Fits! The coal's burning!"

He blinked his teary eyes and focused. A look of horror spread over his face.

"Oh no!" he shouted. "FIRE! *ACHOOO!* FIRE! *ACHOOO!"*

The cry went out through the entire shop.

Soon, all the ogres present were running towards the back, shouting, "Fire! Fire!"

"Get water!" Redbone howled. *"For Grumley's sake, bring water, you clods!"*

The ogres doubled back to the water trough and started scooping out buckets. It was too late, though. The whole coal pile was blazing before the first of them arrived.

Oh boy, I thought, *this isn't good…*

I hoped the fire would stay put, but I hoped in vain. Everything in the shop was covered with coal dust. Wherever sparks touched, fire followed.

Orange flames started climbing the big wooden posts nearby. They went crackling along the solid beams over our heads. The whole place was instantly full of smoke and heat.

Redbone was screaming wildly.

"Save the smithy! Save the smithy!"

Forget the smithy! I thought. *Save ourselves!*

Fits was stumbling around like a blind goat. I grabbed him by the arms and started dragging him backward.

"Come on!" I said. "The whole thing's going up!"

I guided him through the smithy, dodging all the bodies and hot metal in the way. Ash was flying around like confetti. Cinders were stinging my skin. Fits was coughing and sneezing uncontrollably.

"ACHOOO! ACHOOO! ACHOOO!"

I managed to get us out of harm's way. Then I stopped near the entrance where the heat wasn't too bad and stood looking back at the blazing inferno.

Ogres were still dishing water out of the troughs with buckets and running to the back of the shop. But they were way too slow. They'd never be able to put it out.

I suddenly felt burning guilt inside.

This is all my fault, I thought. *I started the fight that led to the fire. Now people might get hurt!*

I desperately wanted to do something to help. But what? We needed way more water to fight a fire like this.

I listened to the big river sloshing beneath the bridge outside. *If only we could bring it right through that door!* I thought. But that was impossible...

Then another idea occurred to me. A brilliant one!

"Stay here!" I said.

I let go of Fits and ran to a nearby rack of tools. I picked up a new, freshly sharpened axe and hefted it in my hands. It felt nice and heavy.

"What are you—*ACHOOO!*—doing?" Fits said.

"Trying to save the smithy," I told him.

I ran over to the cistern and stood looking up at the enormous water tank. There had to be ten thousand gallons in there! We needed every drop. Gripping the axe with both hands, I started looking for a weak spot in the wooden tank.

Fits must have guessed what I was doing. He came staggering over, pinching his nose.

"Wait, wait!" he said. "You can't do that. It'll flood the place!"

"Exactly!" I shouted. "It'll put out the fire!"

"Yeah, but it might drown us all too!"

I considered his point for a moment. But drowning seemed far better than burning to a crisp. I made up my mind.

"You better stand back," I said.

"Aw, man..."

I raised the axe high over my head. Focusing on a gap between the wooden boards, I swung it down as hard as I could.

THWACK!

The metal blade chopped into the wooden tank's side with a big burst of splinters and stuck there. No water came out, though. So, I pulled the axe out with a grunt, raised it over my head, and struck again.

THWACK!

Still nothing.

I freed the axe again. I started chopping at the tank like I was trying to chop down a tree.

THWACK! THWACK! THWACK!

"It's not going to work!" Fits said. "The wood is too thick. Let's just get out of here!"

"I...have...to...try!" I gasped.

My arms felt like rubber. My legs were empty and weak. Still, I raised the axe over my head and summoned all of my strength. I focused on the gash I'd made, preparing for one last effort...

But just then, a little arc of water sprayed out the split wood and squirted over my shoulder. I watched as a stream of water droplets started trickling down the side of the tank.

The cistern let out a deep, menacing groan…

Fits and I looked at each other. It seemed like I'd already done more damage than I thought.

"Should we run?" I said nervously.

"Yeah," Fits answered. "We should run."

I dropped the axe with a clank. We spun around to make a hasty getaway. But I only got two steps in the opposite direction. Then there was a huge cracking sound behind us.

And we were swallowed by a wall of water…

10. Redbone's Wrath

THE TANK EXPLODED like a broken dam! I got tumbled, turned, and tossed. I got plowed and pummeled and beaten. Water went up my nose, into my ears, down my throat. I twirled like a piece of laundry in the spin cycle…

When the beating finally stopped, I found myself staring at the ceiling. I sat up, spewed a fountain from my mouth, and hacked up water until my lungs were clear.

Fits was lying on his side next to me.

"Are you alive?" I said.

He groaned and started to move.

"Unfortunately."

He turned over and coughed for a while. Then he took several long, deep drafts through his nostrils.

"Hey," he said, sniffing. "I think that cured my allergies."

"Well, that's something to be thankful for…"

We sat there looking at the mess around us.

Water and ash lay everywhere in swirling pools. Racks of tools were overturned, and soggy heaps of coal were spread out like black sand dunes. Steam from the doused fires hung everywhere like a mist, making a loud hissing noise in my water-logged ears.

We weren't the only ones recovering from this unnatural disaster. Ogres were coughing and cursing everywhere. I could see dark figures stirring in the fog around us.

"Where's the little blighter that did this?" an ogre grunted somewhere. "I'll *wallop* him!"

I tapped fits with a quivering hand.

"Maybe we should just…slip out while we can," I whispered.

Fits nodded.

"Good thinking."

We got to our knees and started crawling through the steamy haze. I was just trying to figure out which way the exit was when a dark shadow fell over us.

I looked up to find Redbone standing above me. Water was still draining from his bristly beard, and his eyelid was ticking rhythmically. He looked like he'd swallowed a red-hot poker.

"Oh boy," I muttered.

I tried to scramble to my feet. But he bent down in a hurry, grabbed me by the shirt, and hoisted me straight off the ground. He pressed his wet snout to my nose, and I could see the madness in his eyes.

"You…little…brunt," he said. "You *destroyed* my whole bleedin' smithy!"

I grabbed his big red mitts and tried to pry them loose.

"Yeah," I said. "B-but I saved it too!"

"*Saved?!* You call this *saved?!*"

He nodded to the chaos around us. Ogres and trolls were still hoisting their friends off the ground, rubbing bruised shins and aching bones. It looked like a battle had just been fought in here.

"The shop would have completely burned if I hadn't busted the tank," I told him. "It was the only way to put the fires out. I didn't have a choice!"

Redbone's lips pulled back in a sneer.

I thought he'd tear me apart any second now. But somewhere deep down in his warped brain, he must've known I was right because the bitter end never came.

Instead, he dropped me back onto my feet and pointed to the shop entrance with a broken claw.

"Get out," he said, trembling. "Both of you...get out...*now!*"

He didn't have to tell me twice.

I grabbed Fits and jerked him to his feet. Together we started making a mad dash to the exit through the steamy chamber. Ogres growled and barked at us from all sides.

"And don't you ever come back," Redbone howled. *"Or I'll cook you in the forge!"*

Fits hardly said a word as we trudged back to the Pit. He just whimpered to himself and wrung out his tattered shirt.

"Look on the bright side," I said. "At least we got out of work early."

"Yeah! But now we don't have jobs at all!"

Who cares? I thought.

As far as I was concerned, Redbone had gotten what he deserved. That guy was *way* too uptight.

We were just about to start climbing the ramp up to my hutch when a set of footsteps came limping up behind us. I turned to see Fetrol following along, a troubled look on his haggard face.

"Just look at you two," he said. "Wet as mops!"

"We had a little trouble at the smithy today," I started to tell him. But he shook his head impatiently.

"You think I haven't already heard? Everybody's heard! It's the talk of the town!"

"Really? Already?"

For a place that didn't even have light bulbs, word sure traveled fast around here.

"Thoracks sent me to find you," Fetrol

continued. "He wants me to bring you down to his office right away."

"Thoracks?" Fits said. "He's going to eat us!"

Fetrol scratched at a scab on his chin.

"He hasn't eaten anyone in ages," he said uncertainly. "All the same, he's none too pleased. It's best I get you down there as soon as possible. Won't help things to keep him waiting."

"Great. It's one thing after another," I said. "Come on, Fits. Let's get down there before he blows a gasket."

I tried to put on a brave face. But my stomach was balled up in an anxious little knot by the time we arrived at Thoracks' door.

"You'd best wait here," Fetrol said. "I'll go in first, see if I can calm him down a little."

He knocked, let himself in, and closed the door.

Fits and I dawdled in the hallway as minutes slipped away, goblins filing past us. I could just barely hear voices talking inside. Then, there was a terrible crash, followed by a garbled scream.

The door swung open again, and Fetrol leaped out. His eyes were round, and he was holding the doorknob with a shaky hand.

"I did what I could, lads," he said. "But it didn't go too well…he says he wants to see you now."

I sighed.

"Well, thanks for trying, Fetrol," I said.

He gave me a comforting pat on the shoulder. Then, he stepped aside.

A deep, gravelly voice came through the door.

"You two...get in here!"

Fits and I both gulped.

"I guess it's been nice knowing you," I told him.

We pushed through the door to face our fates.

11. Thoracks' Judgment

THORACKS WAS IN the center of the room, his meaty hands folded together and his bullish face twisted with fury. His stone desk was lying in a heap of rubble behind him. I figured that explained the crash we'd heard.

"Shut the door behind you!" he boomed.

Fits closed the door like he was closing his own coffin. We both stood there trembling, our heads bowed.

"First day on the job," Thoracks said to me. "First day! And you burn...down...*the smithy*?!"

"I put it out," I said for the second time.

But Thoracks didn't care.

"Don't give me no blinkin' excuses! I set you up with a cherry of a job, and this is how you repay me? *A raging flood and fire!* In the old days, I'd have been using your bones for toothpicks right now!"

I grimaced, waiting for him to make good on that threat. But he only turned and began pacing the floor, hooves clopping.

"It just so happens you've caught me on a good eon," Thoracks said. "I'm trying to soften my ways. And besides, my digestion just can't handle human meat anymore..."

I looked up, hopeful.

"Does that mean you're letting us off the hook?"

"Ha! You ain't half so lucky!" He had a little triumphant gleam in his eye as he said, "I'm pulling you out of Redbone's shop and putting you on *another* job."

"Whew!" Fits burst out. "Thank Grumley!"

He looked like he'd been given a new chance at life. But Thoracks waved an impatient hand.

"Not you! *You're* going back to the smithy."

"What?! But I can't go back! Redbone hates me now!"

"Too bad. They need you down there," Thoracks said. He did show a little pity, though. "Redbone's a cousin of mine. I'll see he doesn't do anything *too* awful to you. Now, go find Fetrol and have him walk you back."

Fits gave me one last look of despair. With a trembling lip, he turned, opened the big wooden door, and crept back into the hall.

Which just left me…

Thoracks paced behind his broken desk with a big eyebrow raised. A deep growl was gurgling in his throat. He seemed to be thinking about how to deal with me.

After years of getting in trouble, I'd found that the best time to try a bold move was right when things couldn't get any worse. I thought I might even be able to kill two birds with one stone here. I spoke up.

"I guess the best thing to do would be just to let me go," I said with a cheesy smile. "I mean, I can't make any trouble for you in the human world. Right?"

"I had a feeling you'd say that," Thoracks told me. "But you're time here ain't nearly up. You've still got your fair share of work to do. And I reckon there's plenty of places in Dungeonworld you can't make no trouble for me!"

He smiled.

I gulped.

"So…what's it going to be?" I said.

He crossed his arms and tapped a clawed finger against his bottom lip.

"Last time, I gave you the best job I could think of," he said. "This time, I reckon it's only fair you get the *worst* job I can think of. I'm sending you down to The Big Whiff!"

I scrunched my nose.

"The Big Whiff? That doesn't sound so bad."

"That's what you think….I'm putting you on *sewer duty!*"

THE END

Made in the USA
Columbia, SC
11 July 2022

63326663R00071